Mapping Penny's World

For my parents, Grace and Jim,
who showed us the way

And in memory of the real Penny,
the longtime companion of my aunt Lorraine Stewart

Henry Holt and Company, LLC, *Publishers since 1866*
115 West 18th Street, New York, New York 10011

Henry Holt is a registered
trademark of Henry Holt and Company, LLC

Published in Canada by Fitzhenry & Whiteside Ltd.,
195 Allstate Parkway, Markham, Ontario L3R 4T8.

Library of Congress Cataloging-in-Publication Data
Leedy, Loreen.
Mapping Penny's world / by Loreen Leedy
Summary: After learning about maps in school, Lisa maps all the favorite places of her dog, Penny.
[1. Maps—Fiction.   2. Dogs—Fiction.]   I. Title.
PZ7.L51524 Map   2000   [Fic]—dc21   99-48327

ISBN 0-8050-6178-9
First Edition—2000
The artist combined digital painting and photo collage in Adobe Photoshop
to create the illustrations for this book.
Printed in the United States of America on acid-free paper. ∞
1 3 5 7 9 10 8 6 4 2

You can visit Loreen's Web site at
www.loreenleedy.com

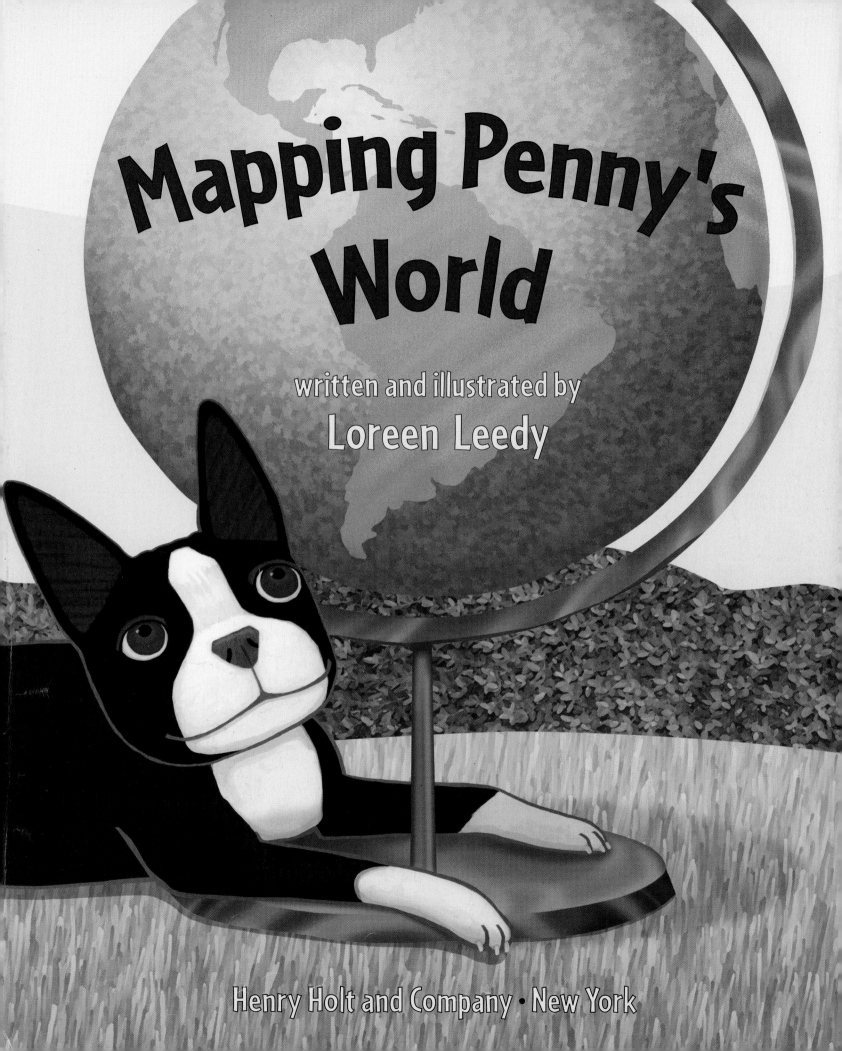

Mapping Penny's World

written and illustrated by
Loreen Leedy

Henry Holt and Company · New York

My name is Lisa, and my class is making maps this month.

My teacher, Mr. Jayson, says a map is a picture of someplace from above. It's like flying over that spot in an airplane.

Mr. Jayson says we can make a map of anyplace—like a room, a yard, or a neighborhood.

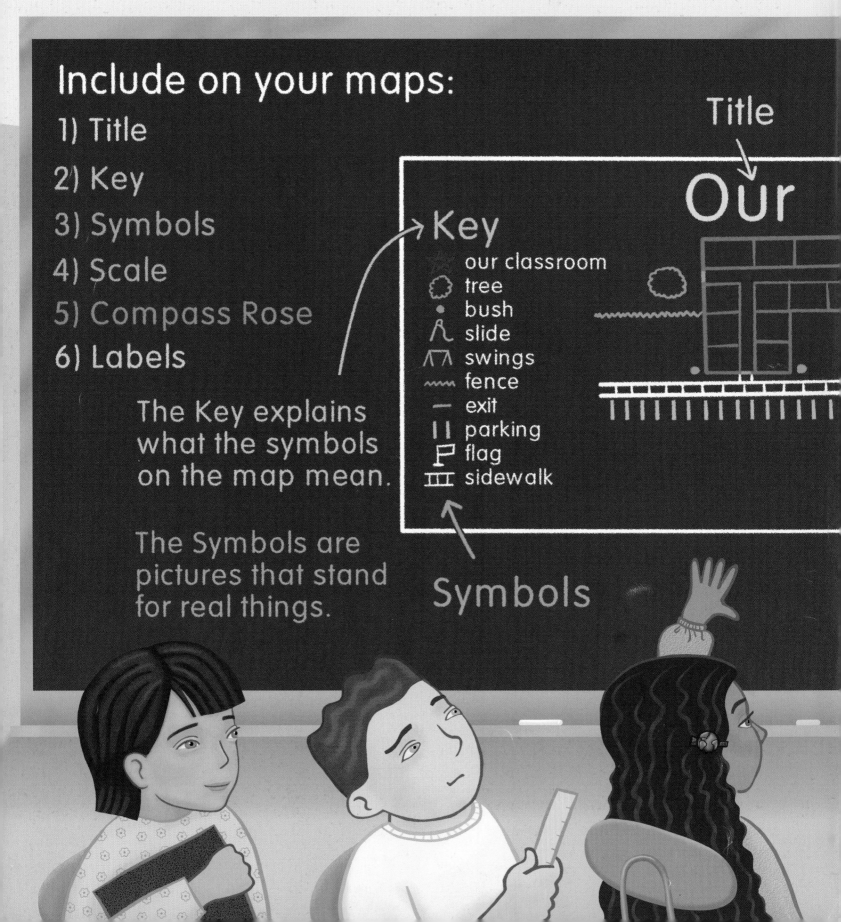

Include on your maps:

1) Title
2) Key
3) Symbols
4) Scale
5) Compass Rose
6) Labels

The Key explains what the symbols on the map mean.

The Symbols are pictures that stand for real things.

Title

Our

Key

☆ our classroom
○ tree
• bush
∧ slide
∧∧ swings
〰 fence
— exit
‖ parking
P flag
Ⅲ sidewalk

Symbols

Maybe I could make a map of my bedroom at home.

I'll measure my room and everything in it to make my map. Of course, I'll have to include Penny's bed. Penny is my Boston terrier and she sleeps in here, too.

Do you want to measure the fish tank, Penny?

My map shows how my bedroom would look from overhead, as if I were looking down from the ceiling.

My Bedroom
by Lisa

bed

rug

plant

bookshelf

That is a close-up map of the fish tank.
Thanks for your help, Penny!

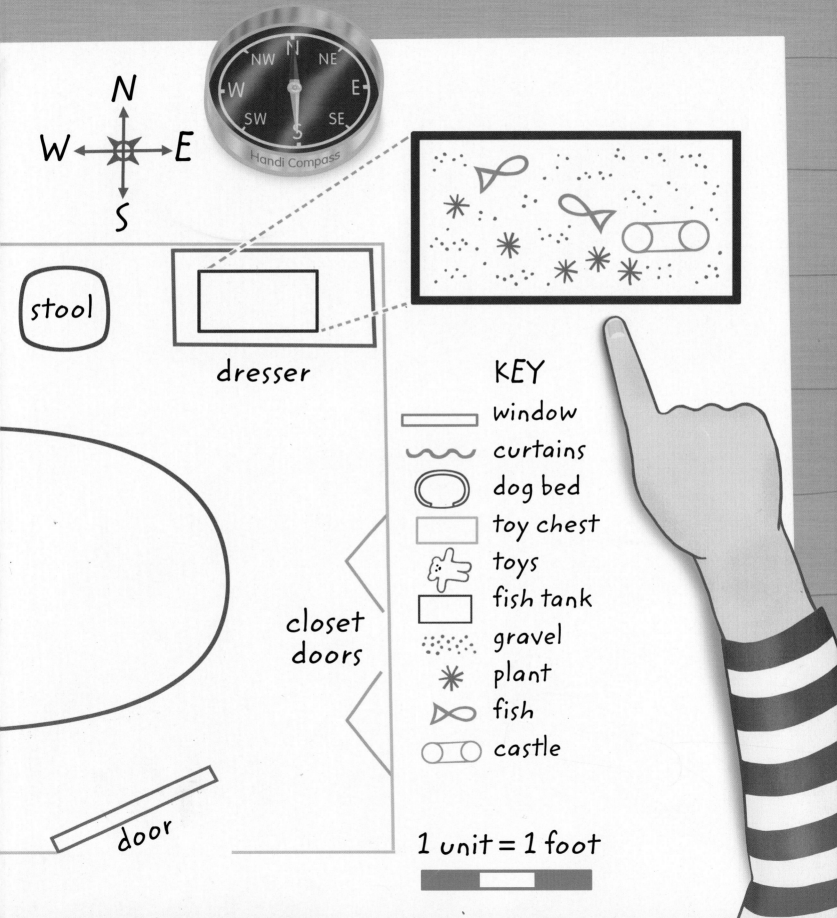

stool

dresser

closet
doors

door

KEY

window

curtains

dog bed

toy chest

toys

fish tank

gravel

plant

fish

castle

1 unit = 1 foot

Penny likes to hide her toys and other stuff in the yard. I have found shoes and socks in the strangest places! Maybe I'll make a map of Penny's hideouts.

On this map, some of the symbols stand for the goodies she has hidden outside. The rest of the symbols represent the fence, table, and other things that are supposed to be out there. Penny, if you hide my doll, you'll be in BIG trouble.

Penny's
KEY
- bone
- squeaky toy
- shoe
- sock
- buried underground
- fence
- birdbath
- stepping-stone
- trash can
- brick path
- table
- chair
- grass
- bush
- cement

Treasure Map

↑ North

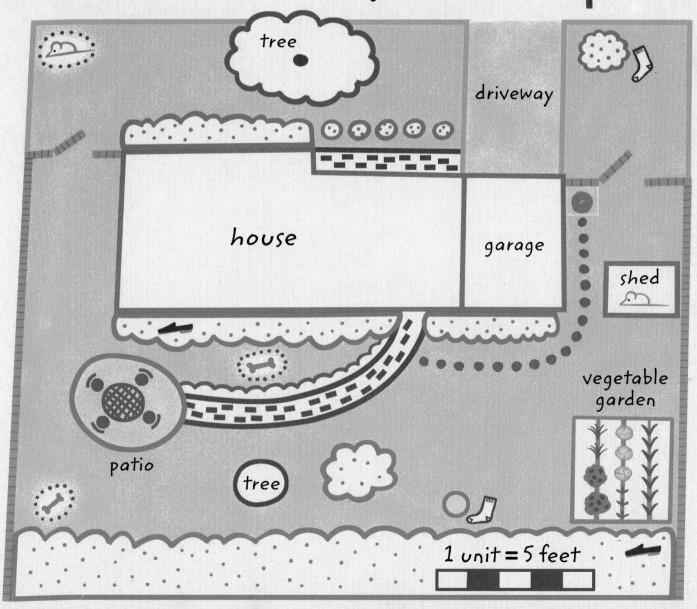

tree

driveway

house

garage

shed

vegetable
garden

patio

tree

1 unit = 5 feet

Maps are good for giving directions. Suppose Penny's friend Maxine wants to come over. You could say, "Go out your back door, turn right by the trash cans, crawl under the gap in the wooden fence (watch out for the big orange cat!), squeeze through the bushes,

turn left, look for the yellow fire hydrant, turn right on the sidewalk, go to the third house on the right with the red door, sit down in front of it, and bark." Whew! Or you could draw a map instead.

Here is the shortest way from Maxine's house to our house.

Maxine's Route

KEY

.... Maxine's path
☐ house
— wood fence
○ trash can
☁ bush
▭ sidewalk
⊙ fire hydrant
🐱 cat

neighbor's house

Maxine's house

Latitude Avenue

It's a lot longer if you go around the block,
instead of going the back way.

I can't take Maxine when I ride my bike, because there's only room for Penny in the basket.

These are our trails. To make this map, I measured our foot paths with a pedometer, a tool that shows how far a person walks. For the bike trails, I used an odometer, which shows how far a vehicle travels.

Our Hike and

KEY

——————— bike trail

– – – – – foot path

~~~~~~~ river

bridge

forest

hill

road

picnic table

R restrooms

River Road

Legend Lake

R

A

STEPCOUNTER
PEDOMETER

0.2 MILES

RESET   SET   MODE

The map's scale shows the real distances in the park. According to the map, the distance between point A and point B is two-tenths of a mile.

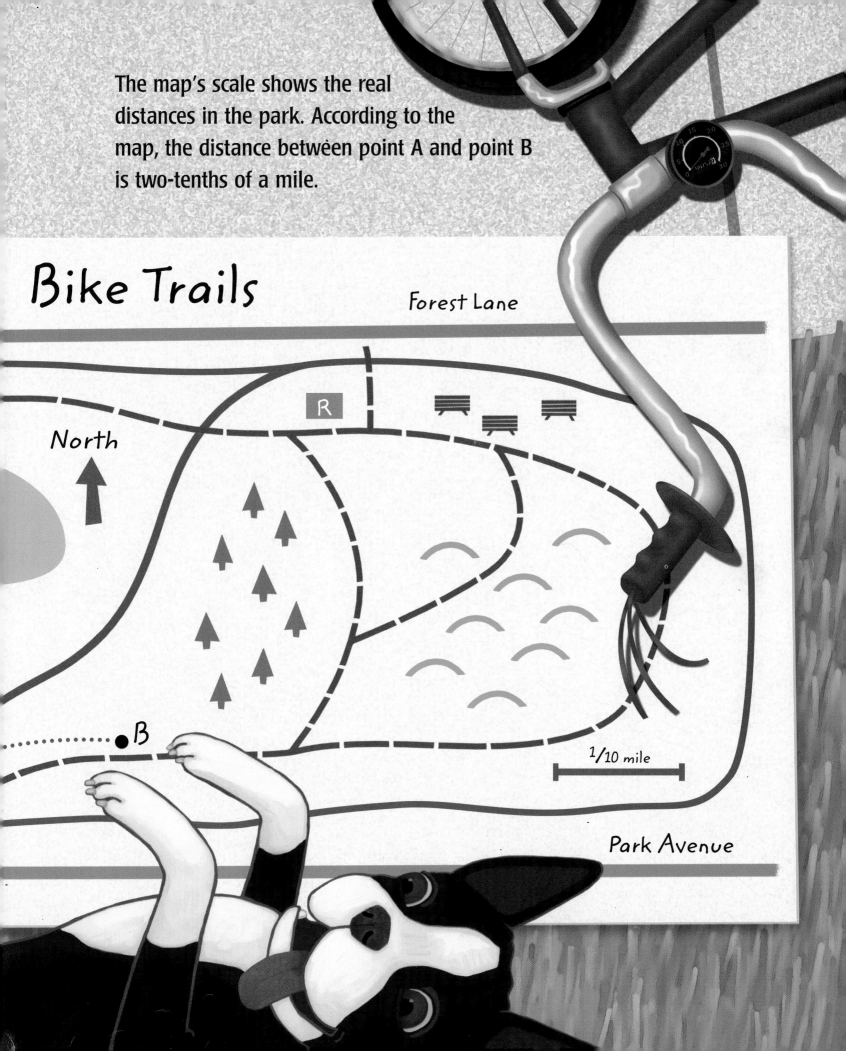

Bike Trails

Forest Lane

R

North

Park Avenue

•B

1/10 mile

When we go out into the neighborhood, Penny has some favorite places she likes to visit again and again.

I made this three-dimensional map with construction paper and clay. The numbers show where Penny can do different activities.

Penny's Favorite Places

Main Street

KEY
1. watch turtles and ducks
2. bark at squirrels
3. beg for new toys
4. smell food
5. meet other dogs
6. rest in the shade
7. fetch sticks

1 unit = 5 feet

Penny loves to travel outside our neighborhood, too. I think there are special places she would enjoy visiting, like a doggie treat factory, a really huge park, or a big dog show.

This map shows a few of the places Penny can go . . .

Penny's Trip

... and I'm going with her.

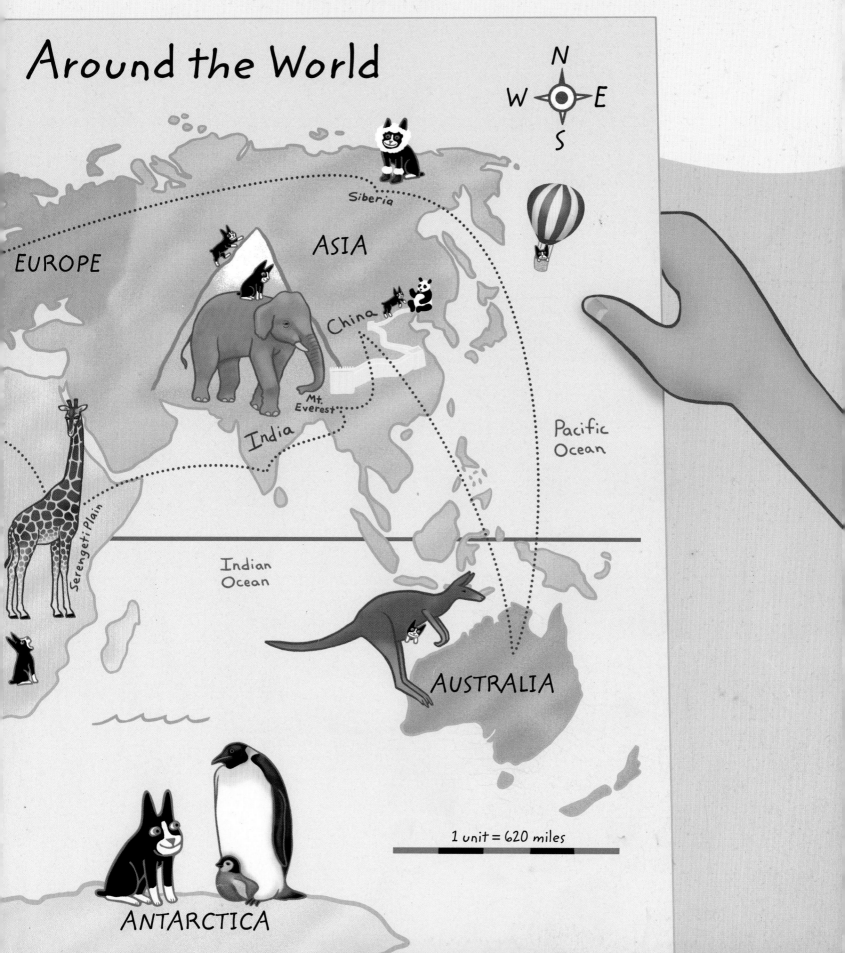

Don't forget the maps, Penny!